KU-593-704

CONTENTS

Years ago, in a distant galaxy, the planet Krypton exploded. Its only survivor was a baby called Kal·El who escaped in a rocket ship. After landing on Earth, he was adopted by the Kents, a kind couple who named him Clark. The boy soon discovered he had extraordinary abilities fuelled by the yellow sun of Earth. He chose to use these powers to help others, and so he became Superman - the guardian of his new home.

DC
SUPER
HEROES

MXY'S MAGICAL MAYHEM

WRITTEN BY
STEVE KORTE

ILLUSTRATED BY
TIM LEVINS

SUPERMAN CREATED BY
JERRY SIEGEL AND
JOE SHUSTER
BY SPECIAL ARRANGEMENT WITH
THE JERRY SIEGEL FAMILY

raintree
a Capstone company — publishers for children

RAINTREE IS AN IMPRINT OF CAPSTONE GLOBAL
LIBRARY LIMITED, A COMPANY INCORPORATED IN
ENGLAND AND WALES HAVING ITS REGISTERED
OFFICE AT 264 BANBURY ROAD, OXFORD, OX2
7DY – REGISTERED COMPANY NUMBER: 6695582

WWW.RAINTREE.CO.UK
MYORDERS@RAINTREE.CO.UK

ART DIRECTOR: BOB LENTZ AND BRANN GARVEY
DESIGNER: HILARY WACHOLZ

ISBN 978 1 4747 3281 9
21 20 19 18 17
10 9 8 7 6 5 4 3 2 1

BRITISH LIBRARY CATALOGUING IN PUBLICATION DATA
A FULL CATALOGUE RECORD FOR THIS BOOK IS AVAILABLE
FROM THE BRITISH LIBRARY.

PRINTED AND BOUND IN CHINA

He is...

CHAPTER 1

AN UNINVITED GUEST

RINNNNNNNNG!

It was 7.30 in the morning in Metropolis when Clark Kent's alarm clock woke him up. Clark groaned. There was an important meeting scheduled for 8.00 a.m. at the *Daily Planet* newspaper where Clark worked as a reporter, and his boss Perry White had warned him not to be late.

But getting ready quickly for work was no problem, because Clark Kent was secretly Superman, the world's most powerful hero.

Clark jumped out of bed. Using his super-speed, he brushed his teeth, combed his hair, showered and gobbled down his breakfast within thirty seconds. That gave Clark almost half an hour to walk to the Daily Planet Building.

Clark was also excited because tonight was the opening night of the Metropolis Carnival. Clark loved to go to the fair and ride the rides. Even though he had amazing superpowers and could fly, he still enjoyed all the thrilling carnival rides as Clark Kent.

In fact, after the meeting today, he was going to ask Perry if he could write a story about the opening of the carnival.

As soon as Clark entered the editorial offices, he heard the booming voice of his boss yelling at him.

"Kent!" Perry yelled. "What did I tell you about being on time for the meeting? It ended two hours ago!"

Clark was confused. He had left his apartment in plenty of time. He looked up at a clock and was shocked to see that it was noon. Clark then took a quick look at his watch, and it also said 12.00.

"Sorry, Chief," he mumbled. "My alarm clock and watch were both, um . . . wrong. Or something." Clark's face was bright red with embarrassment as he sat down at his desk and shuffled some papers, attempting to hide from the grins on his co-workers' faces.

It took Clark a few minutes to work up the courage to go to Perry's office and ask permission to write a story about the carnival. Clark closed the door behind him.

At the desk next to Clark's sat his co-worker and fellow reporter, Lois Lane. She looked up and saw Clark in Perry's office. She couldn't hear Clark's side of the conversation behind the closed door, but she had no trouble hearing Perry's thundering response.

"A carnival story?" Perry scoffed. "Are you out of your mind? Nothing newsworthy ever happens at a carnival. Get back to work, Kent!"

As Clark trudged back to his desk, Lois looked over at him. "Didn't they teach you how to tell the time in Smallville?" she said, then laughed. "It's a good thing you got here in time to have lunch. Or did you forget that we have a lunch date?"

Clark was about to answer, but suddenly his leg kicked out against his will.

THUMP! Clark's foot banged into Lois's chair, knocking her to the ground.

"Ouch!" she cried out. "Clark, just because I made a little joke at your expense doesn't give you the right to kick my chair!"

"I – I don't know what happened, Lois," stammered Clark. "Honestly, it wasn't my fault. I was just about to tell you that I found a great new restaurant called Ben's Bistro that I think you're going to love."

Lois dusted herself off and grabbed her bag. "Well, what are we waiting for?" she asked. "Let's go!"

Clark wasn't sure that he should go to lunch so soon, seeing as he had just arrived at the office, but he didn't want to make Lois any angrier.

"Let's go," he said in agreement.

Lois grabbed Clark's arm and practically pulled him out of the office. "Get a move on, Kent!" she said. "I'm starving."

As they walked outside, Clark couldn't help but notice that it was a gorgeous summer day in Metropolis. His mood began to lighten as he and Lois strolled towards the restaurant. Soon he forgot all about his confusing morning mishaps.

With a smile, Clark pointed to the building as they crossed the street. "Ben's Bistro is right across the street," he said to Lois. "Get ready for a great meal. They have all your favourite dishes."

"Roach poison?" Lois said with disgust. "Is this your idea of a joke, Clark?"

Clark blinked, and then he blinked again.

The restaurant Ben's Bistro that he had seen just a minute ago was now an exterminator shop called Ben's Bug-Stompers! There were giant drawings of cockroaches and rats in the window. Clark shook his head in confusion and began apologizing to Lois.

"Come on, Clark," Lois said. "You've had your fun. Let's just grab a burger next door."

Clark meekly followed Lois into the nearby restaurant. As the two of them sat down at a table, Clark's right arm suddenly flew across the table.

SPLASH! Clark had an astonished look on his face as his hand smacked a jug of water, knocking it over and spilling it all over Lois's dress!

"Something pulled my arm, Lois, and I
–" Clark started to explain, but Lois jumped
to her feet.

"That's it!" she yelled, grabbing her
soaking wet bag. "I don't know what is
wrong with you, Clark, and I just don't
care. You are on your own for lunch!" Clark
watched in dismay as Lois stormed out of
the restaurant.

"What else can go wrong today?" Clark
muttered with his eyes closed.

"Oh, I don't know," said a cheerful
voice from across the table. "The day is still
young."

Clark looked up quickly. There, sitting in
the chair opposite him, was Mr Mxyzptlk,
the magical and mischievous imp from the
Fifth Dimension.

Mr Mxyzptlk loved to torment Superman. Even though Superman had amazing superpowers far beyond those of mortal men, he was helpless against the forces of Mxyzptlk's magic just like everyone else was.

As if things weren't bad enough, Clark suddenly realized that he and his foe were upside-down, with their table and chairs attached to the ceiling. All of the other customers in the restaurant were staring up at them in astonishment.

"Mxy! I might have known," said Clark angrily. "What are you doing here?"

"Oh, just hanging around," he said. Then he chuckled. "I always enjoy visiting your quaint three-dimensional world. Say, are you going to eat that cake?"

Clark looked down – or was it up – at the table and saw a giant chocolate cake in front of him. What was Mxy up to?

"Get us down from here, right now!" Clark demanded. He lunged at Mxy.

"Down? Anything you say!" said the imp as he disappeared in a puff of smoke. Within seconds Clark and the table and chairs all crashed to the ground.

CRASH!

This is a job for – Clark started to say to himself. But just then, the chocolate cake came down and landed with a thud on his head.

SPLATTT!

Clark slowly removed the gooey icing from his face and hair.

BLAM!

A loud crash came from the kitchen. Clark was sure that Mxy was the cause of this new mayhem. As the startled customers watched Clark, he jumped to his feet and ran into the kitchen. There was no chance for him to don his Superman uniform, so Clark Kent would have to deal with the troublesome imp.

What Clark saw when he entered the kitchen caused him to groan with dismay. There was a thick coating of flour covering the walls. Broken eggshells and slabs of butter littered the floor. Rivers of spilled milk poured from ripped-open milk cartons. In the middle of all this destruction stood Mr Mxyzptlk, wearing a giant chef's hat. He waved a giant spatula to greet Clark.

"Hello, Clark Kent," Mxy said with a giggle. "Since you didn't like my chocolate cake, I decided to bake something else for you."

"Mxy, it's time for you to –" Clark began, but he was interrupted by the sound of the oven door crashing open as a giant loaf of bread exploded out of the oven like a cannon ball. The bread crashed into Clark, knocking him over.

"Oof!" said Clark as he hit the floor with a **THUD!**

"Too much yeast, perhaps?" Mxy pondered as another loaf of bread shot out of the oven. It hurtled through the open door and into the restaurant.

"Ouch!" yelled a customer in the restaurant as the bread landed on his head.

WHAM!

Another loaf of bread flew out of the oven and crashed through a window. Then another. And another.

"Is this what you humans call loafing around?" Mxy said as he doubled over with laughter.

Clark quickly looked around to make sure that he and Mxy were alone in the kitchen. Then the quick-thinking reporter ran over to the oven and slammed the oven door shut. Clark removed his glasses, and then he focused his eyes and shot molten-hot rays of heat out of them.

FZZZZZZZZZZZZZZZT!

Clark used his heat vision to melt the edges of the metal oven door and sealed it tightly closed.

No more loaves of bread would shoot out of this oven.

"What a fussy eater you are," Mxy said disapprovingly. "If you don't like my baked goods, maybe I can prepare some seafood for the two of us. Say, that gives me a whale of an idea!"

Suddenly, the tall chef's hat magically transformed into a fishing cap, and the spatula in Mxy's right hand became a fishing rod.

"I think it's time for a little fishing trip," Mxy announced.

POOOOOF!

WOOOOOSH!

The imp disappeared in a cloud of smoke.

Clark Kent shook his head and realized with dismay that his day had just got even worse.

Mr Mxyzptlk was on the loose in Metropolis.

CHAPTER 2
MXY MAYHEM

Clark Kent rushed out of the restaurant and jumped into a dark alley where no one could see him. With super-speed he removed his reporter's suit and revealed his red and blue Superman uniform underneath.

WOOOOOOOOOOSH!

Superman flew high above the buildings of Metropolis. With his super-hearing and X-ray vision, he scanned the buildings below him, searching for any sign of Mr Mxyzptlk.

Superman knew that the incorrigible imp travelled from the Fifth Dimension every 90 days, just to pester him with his magical mayhem. To send Mxy back to the Fifth Dimension, Superman had to trick the pocket-sized prankster into saying or writing his name backwards.

But that was getting harder to do each time that Mxy made a trip to Metropolis.

It didn't take long to spot the tiny troublemaker preparing for his next prank. As the Man of Steel soared above the rooftops of Metropolis, he suddenly heard a high-pitched giggle that sounded just like Mxy's.

"HEE HEE HEE!"

It was coming from the Metropolis Bijou, the largest cinema in town.

Using his X-ray vision to look through several buildings, Superman spied the evil imp skipping into the cinema. Superman swooped down to the cinema with lightning speed, becoming a red-and-blue blur as he zoomed through the foyer.

"Sorry, can't stop to buy a ticket," he said to the startled cashier.

Superman stopped and frowned when he saw the name of the film. It was *A Whale of a Tale*. The Man of Steel had a sinking feeling that Mxyzptlk was about to cause a giant whale-sized problem.

Suddenly, Superman heard cries for help coming from inside the cinema. He also heard the sounds of water splashing and a distressed whale call.

The Man of Steel rushed to open the doors of the cinema and was instantly bombarded with a wall of water crashing down on him and into the foyer. Frantic film fans were swept past him as the water rose in the foyer.

"HELP!"

Everyone was panicking and screaming out to Superman. The Man of Steel darted from person to person, scooping them up and depositing them above the water. The gushing water hit the cinema's till and concessions in the foyer. Machinery parts and popcorn flew through the air.

Superman flew through the foyer, quickly catching each piece of machinery before it could hit someone.

After making sure that the customers and cinema employees were safe, Superman dashed back into the cinema. What he saw there made his jaw drop. Mr Mxyzptlk had caused the cinema screen to come to life, and the room was now flooded with nearly two metres of water.

That was not all, though. A gigantic and very scared humpback whale floated in the water, its tail flukes thrashing and making giant waves!

The whale was explosively exhaling air through the blowhole on top of its head. Sitting above the blowhole, bobbing up and down with an evil grin on his face, was Mr Mxyzptlk. He was wearing a bright yellow raincoat and seemed to be really enjoying himself.

"Hey, Superman," Mxy called out, "it looks like something fishy has happened here. I hope you don't think I did this on porpoise!" With that, Mxy doubled over in a fit of giggles.

"As usual, you're not funny and not very clever," said the Man of Steel. "Whales are mammals, not fish. And this one doesn't belong in a cinema any more than you belong in Metropolis!"

"Tell me more, you big bore . . ." began Mxy, but before he could finish his sentence Superman used his super-breath.

WOOOOOOOOOOOOSH!

The blast knocked the imp from his perch, sending him somersaulting through the air into the foyer. Superman continued to exhale with all his strength.

FWOOOOOOOOSH! Mxy tumbled down the cinema's escalators with many loud thumps, finally landing in a large dustbin outside the cinema.

"You haven't heard the last of me!" Mxy screeched – just before a giant lid crashed onto his head with a **CLANG!**

"Now that I've taken out the rubbish, my next job is to get this frightened whale to safety," said Superman.

Using his super-strength, the Man of Steel lifted the whale as gently as possible and cradled the giant mammal above him as he flew it far beyond the shores of Metropolis.

SPLASSSSSSH! The humpback whale was safe and sound. With a happy wave of its tail, the whale dived deep into the waters.

But the Man of Steel wasn't able to rest for long.

"Superman! Help! Help!" a voice cried out.

It was Lois Lane! Superman would know her voice anywhere.

WOOOOOOOOOSH! The Man of Steel flew towards the sound of Lois's voice. When he arrived, he found Lois in her car, frantically pumping the brakes, trying to slow down as she zoomed backwards down the streets of Metropolis. Fortunately, no one had been hurt yet, but there wasn't a second to lose.

Superman quickly grabbed the front of the car and brought it to a screeching stop.

"Hey! What's the big idea?" came a familiar squeaky voice from under the car.

Of course, it was Mr Mxyzptlk. "Go away, Muscles," Mxy said. "You bother me!"

Mxy sneered at the Man of Steel as he emerged from beneath the car. "I didn't like what Miss Lane wrote about me in the *Daily Planet*," Mxy explained, "so I thought it was time to put her in reverse. I suppose you could call it an unlucky brake!" Mxy started giggling again.

"What in the world," Lois said angrily. She climbed out of the car and started swinging her bag in the air.

POOF! Mr Mxyzptlk disappeared before she could hit him. *BLAM!* Lois's bag smashed into Superman's head!

"What's the big idea?" she yelled. "I could have been killed. What were you doing to my car? And who are you?"

Lois continued to smack Superman with her bag.

Superman was shocked that Lois did not recognize him. Lois did not know that he was secretly Clark Kent, but she had written many stories about Superman. She and Superman were friends. One day, Superman hoped they'd be even more. But right now, it seemed like she didn't even know who he was!

"Miss Lane, I can explain!" **SMACK!** "Lois, please stop hitting me with your bag! I'm your friend –" **SMACK!** "I'm Superman!" he said.

Just then a policeman came running over.

"What's going on here?" he asked Lois. "Is this man bothering you?"

"He did something to my car," said Lois. "And he claims to know me. I'll admit that he looks very handsome in that uniform, but I've never seen him before!"

Turning to Superman, the policeman said, "What's with the acrobat suit? Are you from the circus? I have a good mind to give you a ticket for blocking traffic!"

"Stop joking around, officer," said the Man of Steel. "You know I'm Superman!"

"Never heard of you," the policeman said firmly. "Is that your first name or last name? I'm going to need to see some identification."

"You've never heard of me?" Superman said with disbelief. "Are you new to the police force?"

"Twenty years this June," said the officer, "and I don't know any Superman!"

"I saw the whole thing, officer," cried out a man from across the street. "The guy in the red and blue pyjamas jumped out of nowhere and started pushing her car backwards. He's crazy!"

This is Mxy's doing, realized Superman. *The troublesome imp must have magically erased all the memories of Superman from these people.*

That meant that, somehow, Superman would have to prove that he was the Man of Steel. Looking across the street, Superman saw an abandoned building.

"To prove my powers, I'll smash through that concrete wall," he said to the disbelieving crowd of people.

He turned back to the gathered crowd to say: "And then, of course, I will repair any damage to the building."

With a lunge, Superman launched himself at the building. **CRUNCH!** He crashed through the concrete and left a gaping hole.

That should convince them, he said to himself. But when he emerged from the building, he was astonished to see that everyone standing around Lois's car was laughing at him.

"If you're a circus strongman, you're going to have to do better than to knock a hole in a condemned building," said Lois with a smile.

Superman quickly turned around and saw a giant sign on the wall.

The sign read: *Danger! Condemned Building. Unsafe. Metropolis Department of Public Safety.*

Superman was sure that sign had not been on the building two minutes ago. It was more of Mxy's magic!

"Can a circus strongman fly?" demanded Superman with exasperation. Crouching down, he made a mighty leap into the air and soared above the heads of the crowd. This would convince them for sure! Then Superman heard even louder laughter below him.

"Very funny," called out the policeman. "We can see that jet pack on your back and the springs on the bottom of your feet!"

What the heck is going on? Superman thought.

Sure enough, strapped to the bottoms of his boots were two giant springs, and beneath his red cape was a shiny metallic jet pack. Mxy had tricked him again.

POOF! Mr Mxyzptlk was suddenly floating in the air next to Superman.

"Lovely day for a flight, don't you think?" said Mxy. "And isn't this the funniest prank that has ever happened in any dimension? You have spent years helping people and making yourself famous. And I made the whole city forget you in a single second!"

"Hilarious," said Superman glumly.

"Well, now I'll let you sit and stew," said Mxy. "I have to go back to the Fifth Dimension. I'm running for president of the Anti-Superman Club, and I have to be there for the election."

"You're going back without removing your amnesia spell?" Superman asked with concern. "How will I be able to fight crime if no one trusts me or knows who I am?"

"That's what makes this the best prank ever!" Mxy said.

Mxy roared with laughter, then spoke faster than a normal human could hear. "In the past you've always had to trick me into going back to the Fifth Dimension. But this time I want to go back, and you want me to stay here! As long as I don't say my name backwards, all of my magical mischief will stay in place. So goodbye for now!"

"Wait!" Superman called out. He had an idea how he could trick Mr Mxyzptlk into saying his name backwards.

"Don't you want the people of Metropolis to know that you did this to me?" Superman asked. "You could be more famous than I ever was!"

Mxy tilted his head. Superman could tell the little imp had taken the bait. "Let me splash your name all over the city," the Man of Steel continued. "It will only take a few minutes with my super-speed. The name 'Mr Mxyztplk' will be on everybody's lips!"

"You're right," Mxy said firmly. "I should be famous! Only my name is Mxyzptlk."

"My apologies," said Superman humbly. "Watch me as I go into action!"

Superman zipped over to the city dump as Mxy followed close behind.

WOOOOOOOOSH!

The Man of Steel grabbed a fridge-sized metal boiler from a heap of rubble. Steam was still coming out of the boiler. He lifted the bulky machine into the air and began writing giant letters made out of steam in the sky.

M-X-Y-Z-T-P-L-K formed in the air.

"You're spelling it wrong! It's Mxyzptlk!" squeaked Mxy. "Swap the 'T' and the 'P' around!"

"I'm so sorry," said Superman. "Come with me to the botanical gardens. I'll get it right this time."

At the gardens, Superman zoomed over to a giant hedge. Red laser beams shot out of his eyes as he used his heat vision to carve giant letters out of the shrubs.

ZRRRRT! ZRRRRRRRRRRRRRRRT!

M-X-Y-Z-T-L-P-K was the leafy green result.

"It's not spelled that way," cried Mxy as he hopped up and down in anger. "It's Mxyzptlk!"

"Hmmm, I'm usually much better at spelling," Superman said with feigned embarrassment. "Let me try again."

Next Superman painted a giant billboard on top of the Metropolis Bus Station. It read, "M-X-Z-Y-T-K-L-P."

"What a dunce you are!" said Mxy with disgust. "How many times do I have to tell you that it's Mxyzptlk!"

"I do apologize. Give me one more chance," said Superman as he zoomed into the air and flew over to the hills on the west side of Metropolis.

On a steep, rocky ledge, the Man of Steel carved out the letters K-L-T-P-Z-Y-X-M into the rock.

It was the imp's name backwards. If he could trick Mr Mxyzptlk into reading those letters out loud, the pint-sized prankster would disappear back to the Fifth Dimension for another 90 days, and the magical amnesia spell he had cast over Metropolis would be broken.

"Mxy, did I get it right this time?" Superman called out. "Mxy? Where are you?"

But the impudent imp was nowhere to be seen. He had lost patience with Superman's many misspellings of his name.

CRASSSSSSSSSH!

Oh no, thought Superman, *what is Mxy up to now?*

CHAPTER 3

RUNAWAY TRAINS

Within minutes Superman discovered
Mr Mxyzptlk's next mission of mischief.

Above the streets of Metropolis, far
on the east side, was the city's only
remaining elevated subway train track.
It was a charming and ornate structure
that had originally been built in the early
1900s, and subway riders enjoyed the
panoramic views as the trains travelled
high above the streets.

Today was no exception, and the trains were packed with tourists and citizens of Metropolis.

Superman zoomed through the city. He used his super-hearing to determine that the loud crash had come from the area near the elevated train tracks.

WOOOOOOOOOOSH!

Faster than a speeding bullet, Superman flew to the east side of Metropolis. There he saw Mxy wearing a welder's mask on his face. The imp was holding a giant flaming blowtorch in his hands.

FZZZZT! FZZZZZZT! Sparks flew into the air as he cut holes in the intricate metalwork of the elevated train tracks. Mxy was also welding the tracks, knocking big holes in them and pushing the safety rails over the side.

CRUNCH! A giant metal wall crashed to the ground.

"I'd say I am on track for my best prank ever," Mxy said proudly. "Do you follow my train of thinking? Get it? Train? Track?"

Before Superman could knock the blowtorch from the mischievous imp's hands, Mr Mxyzptlk lifted one hand to his ear. "Is that a train whistle I hear?" he asked with a satisfied smile. "Or could it be two?"

Superman heard a sharp train whistle behind him. Whipping around, he saw a subway train hurtling down the tracks, heading right for them. It was packed with passengers.

Suddenly he heard a second train whistle.

Two trains were coming from opposite directions! Superman realized. Mxy had cut both tracks, leaving gaping holes in them high above the ground. When the trains reached the end of the tracks, they would go sailing over the edge and crash below.

And the trains were going to arrive within minutes!

ZRRRRRT! ZRRRRRT! Thinking fast, Superman used his heat vision to turn the tracks to volcanic-hot metal. He quickly joined the two tracks together. Mr Mxyzptlk was watching with a puzzled look on his face.

"Um, I wonder if you are aware that that the two trains are going to crash into each other," Mxy said. "Not that it matters to me, of course."

Ignoring the pesky prankster, Superman flew through the air. He was heading for the first train as it hurtled towards him. The Man of Steel planted his feet on the track and reached out to grab the engine at the front of the train.

SCREEEEEEEEEEEEEEEEEECH!

Sparks flew in the air as Superman tried to stop the train. The train track below Superman's feet splintered and pieces went flying into the air.

As Superman used all his strength to push the train, the tracks below him wobbled dangerously.

SCREEEEEEEEEEEEEEEEEEECH!

Finally, the train squealed to a halt. The happy passengers cheered for the Man of Steel, but there was no time to rest.

The other train was coming closer. As Superman turned around to stop the second train, he was dismayed to see that Mr Mxyzptlk had not been idle. The magical imp had knocked a gaping hole in the tracks again. There was no time to repair the track.

Like a superpowered missile, Superman launched himself towards the train. Just as it was about to go over the edge of the tracks, the Man of Steel dived under the first carriage. It took all his strength, but Superman pushed up, up and away, lifting the train above him and into the air.

The Man of Steel's muscles strained as he worked to carry the train and fly at the same time. Connected to each other, the carriages lifted off the tracks, and soon the entire train was sailing through the air.

The Man of Steel was working hard to keep it aloft. As gently as possible, Superman guided the entire train safely to the ground. The passengers had been shaken up and knocked around, but no one was seriously hurt.

While Superman was helping the passengers off the trains, Mr Mxyzptlk was hopping up and down in anger.

"You're always spoiling all my fun!" he yelled. Just then, he spotted the bright lights of the Metropolis Carnival fair grounds off in the distance.

Hmmm, Mxy thought to himself, *Superman can stop my tricks one at a time. I wonder what would happen if he had to deal with a whole carnival full of my kind of fun.*

"I suppose there's only one way out," Mxy said with a giggle as he flew towards the fairground. "All's fair in war, after all!"

/AL CHAOS

The sound of a carnival organ filled the air, along with the yells and laughter of people enjoying the fair. Even though it was night-time, the sky was bright with the lights of the carnival rides.

Tonight, the park was completely filled with customers, and Mr Mxyzptlk was clapping his hands in delight at the thought of all the mischief he could cause for them.

Superman is probably not far behind me, he thought to himself, pondering how best to cause the most amount of trouble.

Then an idea popped into his head! *I can turn myself into a brightly coloured balloon,* he thought. *Who would ever notice one stray balloon floating around the fairground?*

POP! Mr Mxyzptlk magically transformed himself into a balloon. Floating above the carnival, his grinning face filled the balloon. Squeaky giggles emanated from the balloon as he fitfully plotted his next tricks.

Superman arrived minutes later, soaring over the fairground in search of his foe. The Man of Steel looked nervously at all the carnival attractions.

Superman knew that Mxy would not hesitate to magically transform a ride for his own evil purposes.

All that Superman could do was react to each problem as it occurred, and hope that he could find a way to trick Mr Mxyzptlk into saying his name backwards.

Until that point, as frustrating as it was to admit, Superman was completely subject to Mxy's chaotic whims.

Superman didn't notice the Mxy balloon as it floated near the King Snake roller coaster, a giant ride with a train of green cars shaped just like a snake. It was the biggest roller coaster at the fair, and its happy riders shrieked with delight as the snake-shaped cars zoomed along the tracks.

"Those dim-witted people are having a lot of fun on that stupid snake-themed roller coaster," said Mxy. "I wonder if they would enjoy it as much if they were riding on top of a real snake. Let's give it a try, shall we?"

POP! POP! POP! Mr Mxyzptlk magically transformed the roller coaster cars into an enormous green snake slithering over the tracks!

"EEEEK!" several voices cried.

The startled riders on the roller coaster suddenly found themselves hanging on to a giant writhing and hissing green serpent. The head of the snake whipped around, baring its gleaming fangs as it prepared to bite its unlucky passengers.

HISSSSSSSSSSSSSSSSSS!

Superman arrived just as the snake was about to grab one of the riders.

KA-RAAAAAAAAACK!

The Man of Steel smacked the snake hard on its snout, causing the serpent to pull back. Superman let out a sigh of relief, and prepared to do battle with the snake.

Unfortunately, the impact also caused the snake to shake its entire body, which meant that the roller coaster passengers went flying into the air!

ZOOOOM!

WOOOSH!

SWOOOSH!

Superman zoomed into action, grabbing each person just before he or she hit the ground.

When all the passengers were safely on the ground, Superman leapt into the air again and wrapped his mighty arms around the giant, hissing snake.

HISSSSSSSSSSSS! CLANK!

The serpent tried to sink its fangs into the Man of Steel, but Superman's skin was invulnerable.

While the snake busied itself with attempting to bite the Man of Steel, he tugged on its tail and wrapped it around the rest of its body.

HISSSSSSSS! The snake whined as Superman coiled it tighter and tighter around the roller coaster tracks. Soon, the snake could no longer move.

"Help! Help!" a voice cried out. "Help me, please!"

While Superman was dealing with the angry snake, Mr Mxyzptlk had been causing even more chaos. The Wild Octopus ride had come to life!

No longer was it a carnival ride with several cables connected to cars that flew gently up and down. Due to the magic of Mr Mxyzptlk, it had become a giant purple octopus!

ROAAAAAAAAAAAAAR!

The monstrous beast sent its eight arms outwards, waving them menacingly in the air. Caught in the grip of one of those tentacles was a terrified young man, screaming for help.

AHHHHHHHHHHHHHHHHHHH!

Superman flew over to the octopus and grabbed its arm.

Superman struggled mightily to try to free the young man. With a powerful tug, Superman pulled the man loose, but just then the octopus ensnared the Man of Steel within its other arms.

Seven long octopus tentacles wrapped around Superman's chest and legs, squeezing him tightly. Superman watched helplessly as one of the octopus's arms moved closer and closer towards his face.

POP! POP! The suction cups on that arm quickly covered Superman's mouth and nose. Now he could not breathe!

Even though his mouth and nose were covered, Superman was still able to use his eyes to blast the octopus with his heat vision.

ZAP! ZAP!

The octopus loosened its grip on the Man of Steel, allowing him to wriggle free of the creature's grasp. As the octopus thrashed in anger, Superman grasped one of its arms, and then another.

WOOOOOOOOOOOOOSH!

Superman began swinging the octopus in circles high in the air. Then he released it. **WOOOOOOOOOOOOOSH!** It sailed over half the city and landed with a giant splash in a tank at the Metropolis Aquarium.

"What next," Superman said grimly as he soared over the carnival. "I'm really getting sick of Mr Mxyzptlk."

POP! The balloon that was floating near Superman exploded, and there was Mr Mxyzptlk hovering in the air next to him.

"I thought I would give you fair warning," Mxy said, and then he burst into laughter. "Stop! I'm too funny. Fair warning. At the fair! Does it get any better?"

Superman angrily grabbed the little man by his collar and said, "You've had your fun, but you've put too many people in danger for one day. It's time for you to go home!"

"But the fun has just begun," Mxy said. "These solo pranks are enjoyable, but I think we both need a challenge. I wonder what would happen if all the carnival attractions came to life at the same time? Can one Man of Steel stop every monster? Let's find out!"

With that, Mr Mxyzptlk disappeared in a puff of pink smoke.

Superman stared down at the carnival in dismay. Below him was total mayhem.

The giant skeleton statue outside the House of Horrors had come to life and was stomping through the fairground, waving its axe at the frightened crowd.

A clown-shaped dustbin was chasing a man, nibbling at him as he ran from it.

The horses on the merry-go-round had all magically come to life and were trying to kick the passengers or stab them with their unicorn horns.

The bumper cars careered out of their enclosure, smashing into each other and knocking over anything in the way.

And the soft toy prizes were jumping from ride to ride, throwing food and drinks at people.

Superman flew into action. He landed in front of the giant skeleton.

WOOOOOOOOOOOSH! The skeleton swung its razor-sharp axe at the Man of Steel, missing him by just a few centimetres. As the skeleton raised its axe again, Superman used his super-breath to freeze the giant foe before he could strike again. **KIRRRRRRRRRRRSH!** Superman then flew faster and faster around the skeleton, trapping the creature in a violent whirlwind.

CLINK! CLANK! CLUNK! The fierce winds caused the skeleton to collapse, its dry bones clattering onto the ground.

Superman then zapped the clown-shaped dustbin and bumper cars with his heat vision, melting them into piles of rubble.

The Man of Steel raced over to the merry-go-round and flew the frightened passengers to safety. He then gathered up a giant rope and lassoed the angry merry-go-round horses, herding them into a pen to keep them separated from the citizens.

BONKKKKKK! A wooden bowling pin bounced off the Man of Steel's head. A soft-toy monkey had come to life and was methodically hurling heavy bowling pins at him.

Looking up, Superman saw that all of the soft toys from the carnival were scampering on wires high above the ground. Their arms were laden with balls and balloons!

ZOOOOOOOOM! Superman quickly gathered up all the misbehaving toys and threw them into a cage.

Even as Superman solved each problem, three or four new ones popped up. He knew he couldn't be everywhere at once!

Or can I? he wondered.

It would take several Supermen to handle all the problems that Mxy had caused.

That gave Superman an idea.

CHAPTER 5

MIRROR MISCHIEF

Tucked into a far corner of the fairground was the House of Mirrors. Superman zoomed into the air and flew towards it. *WOOOOOOOOOOOSH!*

"Hey Superman, come back and play," called out Mxy with a laugh. "I didn't think you would give up so easily!"

Superman ignored the taunts of his foe and stepped into the House of Mirrors. Standing before him were many distorted Superman mirror reflections. Some were short and stout.

Other reflections were stretched and skinny. A few others were all zigzagged with bodies like wavy lines. One reflection had a giant head that took up half his body.

Superman had to smile for just a moment at the funny reflections. "Thanks to Mxy's magic, everything in the carnival has come to life," he said to his reflections. "Shouldn't you all come to life, too?"

POOF! POOF! POOF! With flashes of magic, all of the reflections of Superman stepped out from the mirrors, facing the one-and-only original Man of Steel. It was an unusual-looking group of heroes, and they stood at attention, awaiting instructions from Superman.

"The carnival is in danger," the Man of Steel told them. "And it's up to us to save everyone."

"It's a good thing you thought of us," shouted the Superman reflections in unison. "This looks like a job for *Supermen!*"

With that, the group of superpowered heroes flew out of the House of Mirrors, ready to deal with Mxy's carnival capers.

Several of the reflections zapped roaring animals with super-breath, freezing their paws so they couldn't move. Then they moved the animals to cages and pens and gently defrosted them with their lightest heat vision. Others smashed the rampaging zombies and vampires and other monsters that had emerged from the House of Horrors. Still more captured roving rides as they stomped across the fairground and menaced the customers. As each ride whirred to life, a Superman arrived to stop it.

Others escorted the crowds of people to safety. Before long, the fairground was quiet except for the sounds of grumbling from the rides and attractions that had been tightly tied up or stuffed into cages.

POP! With a burst, Mr Mxyzptlk suddenly appeared beside Superman. "That wasn't fair," he said with a scowl. "You used my own magic against me!"

"That's true," said the Man of Steel. "And now there are lots of me to fight your magical mischief. How are you going to deal with that?"

Mxy frowned at the thought of all the superpowered foes. *One Superman is too many,* he thought glumly.

"I do have an idea that might help you," said Superman, slowly. "But you probably won't like it."

Mr Mxyzptlk tried to pretend that he was not interested. "No, I probably won't like it, but go ahead and tell me anyway," he said.

"Well," said Superman, "I was thinking that we could go to the House of Mirrors, and you could use your magic to make my reflections disappear. I would be so grateful that I would be willing to put up a sign in there describing what you had done so that everyone could see how clever you are. And this time I should be able to spell your name correctly."

Mxy was delighted with the idea. Not only would he get rid of all the Supermen, but also his exploits would be on display for all to see.

"I'll do it!" he declared with a joyous giggle.

Superman called to the other Supermen to follow him and Mr Mxyzptlk into the House of Mirrors. With a wave of his hands, the magical imp caused the reflections to disappear back into the mirrors.

"Now, how about that sign?" Mxy said.

Superman had his back to Mxy, and without turning around he brought out a giant sign that read, "This is where MR MXYZPTLK defeated SUPERMAN." With a smile, he held it up to the mirror.

Mxy looked at the sign in the mirror. With a frown on his face he tried to read the backward lettering.

"What does 'KLTPZYXM' mean?" he started to say, before he realized that he had been tricked into saying his name backwards.

POOF!

Mr Mxyzptlk disappeared, this time for good. The reflections were gone, and the carnival had returned to normal.

Superman emerged from the Hall of Mirrors and looked around. Suddenly the carnival rides did not look as entertaining to him. *And the boss says that nothing newsworthy ever happens at carnivals!* he said to himself.

The Man of Steel smiled as he flew towards home.

MISTER MXYZPTLK

Real Name:
Unpronounceable

Occupation:
Professional nuisance

Base:
The Fifth Dimension

Height:
1.10 metres

Weight:
27 kilograms

Eyes:
Black

Hair:
White

Mr Mxyzptlk, or Mxy for short, is a mischievous imp from
the Fifth Dimension. In this wacky world, everyone has
strange magical powers. Unfortunately, Mxy likes using
his terrible tricks to torment his greatest foe. Every 90 days,
he travels to Earth and tries to humiliate Superman with
his pathetic pranks. Fortunately, the Man of Steel knows
exactly how to get rid of the puny pest – at least for a
while.

- To send Mr Mxyzptlk back to the Fifth Dimension, Superman must trick the miniature magician into saying or writing his name backwards.

- Mr Mxyzptlk's strange name is pronounced "Mix-yez-pittle-ick".

- Only a few people know that Clark Kent is really the Man of Steel. Mxy is one of them.

- Superman also has some weaknesses. The Man of Steel cannot defend himself against magic. He's often helpless against the tiny trickster's spells.

BIOGRAPHIES

STEVE KORTE is a freelance writer. At DC Comics he
edited over 500 books. Among the titles he edited are 75
Years of DC Comics, winner of the 2011 Eisner Award,
and Jack Cole and Plastic Man, winner of the 2002
Harvey Award. He lives in New York, USA, with his own
super-cat, Duke.

TIM LEVINS is best known for his work on the Eisner
Award-winning DC Comics series, Batman: Gotham
Adventures. Tim has illustrated other DC titles, such
as Justice League Adventures, Batgirl, Metal Men and
Scooby Doo, and has also done work for Marvel Comics
and Archie Comics. Tim enjoys life in Ontario, Canada,
with his wife, son, puppy and two horses.

GLOSSARY

carnival public celebration, often with rides, games and parades

dimension different place in space and time

disbelief refusal to believe something

feigned pretended

frantic wildly excited by worry or fear

imp little devil or demon known for being mischievous

loafing spending time doing little or nothing

mayhem situation of confusion or violent destruction

mischief playful behaviour that may cause annoyance or harm to others

mishaps unfortunate accidents

prankster someone who plays mischievous or playful tricks on others

DISCUSSION QUESTIONS

1. Mxy loves to play tricks on the Man of Steel. What tricks have you played on others, or have others played on you? Talk about it.

2. Clark Kent is a reporter at the *Daily Planet*. Would you like to be a reporter? Why or why not?

3. This book has ten illustrations. Which one is your favourite? Why?

WRITING PROMPTS

1. Design your own carnival ride. What type of ride is it? Why is it fun to ride on? Write about it, then draw a picture of your carnival creation.

2. What was your favourite trick that Mxy played on Superman? Write about it.

3. Write another chapter to this story. What happens to Mxy? Is Superman able to stop the mischievous little imp, or does he manage to get away? You decide.

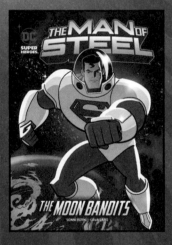